Blessed to Be Free

Blessed to Be Free

After Wrongful Imprisonment

Keith E. Benjamin

Library of Congress Control Number:		2018911300
ISBN:	Hardcover	978-1-9845-5468-0
	Softcover	978-1-9845-5467-3
	eBook	978-1-9845-5466-6

Print information available on the last page.

Rev. date: 04/29/2019

To order additional copies of this book, contact:
Xlibris
1-888-795-4274
www.Xlibris.com
Orders@Xlibris.com
762614

CONTENTS

This narrative is written about Mr. Mawuli B. and tells of his life and experience of wrongful imprisonment for a murder he claimed he did not commit. It tells how the local government of a small Caribbean island used perjury, tampered with crucial evidence, and paid their star witness to provide false testimony that led to his conviction of first-degree murder and, subsequently, to his being sentenced to life in prison without the possibility of parole.

It gives a glimpse of a court system governed by the United States' principles—a court system that does not always accept the truth after they have convicted a person, a court system that sometimes turns a deaf ear even when evidence presented proves a person was wrongfully convicted or denied a fair trial.

This memoir is dedicated to the men and women who were or who are still innocently imprisoned. It is dedicated to the families, organizations, and individuals who seek justice for the wrongfully and innocently imprisoned. It is also a lesson to show how easy it is to be imprisoned and that though innocent, it is extremely difficult to regain your freedom.

In my preparation for this memoir, I had several discussions with and heard from innocent men and women of how clear evidence were presented to the courts and how their motions for release on the grounds of their innocence were denied by the courts. Some of these individuals served time and were released after years, in spite evidence of their innocence. There were some who were blessed to be freed by a parole board and some by way of executive relief. In the case of release by the parole board or executive relief, the innocent individuals retained prison records. Though these individuals may be innocent, in the eyes of society, they are still considered guilty because of the prison records hanging over their heads.

I often wonder why it is so hard to obtain freedom from a wrongful conviction, particularly when the evidence of innocence is before the courts. Perhaps it is hard for people to admit their wrongdoing, regardless of the negative impact on one's life.

This memoir talks about a man, Mawuli B., who presented facts and evidence of his innocence to the courts, but his motion for release was denied for years. After the review of Mr. Mawuli B.'s case by the executive branch of his local Caribbean island, it was revealed and accepted that he was not given a fair trial. His conviction was upheld, but his sentence was commuted to time served. After twenty-five years of wrongful imprisonment, Mr. Mawuli B. was *blessed to be free.*

His Early Life

Mawuli B. was born on September 28, 1957, in New York. He was raised on a small Caribbean island just thirty-two square miles. Mawuli was raised by his father and his stepmother, who reared him from childhood to adulthood. Both his father and stepmother, as well as his biological mother, were all of Caribbean descent. He was separated from his biological mother at a very young age after his father and mother separated. The separation from his mother at a young age left him with a very vague recollection of her. Mawuli and his father migrated from New York to the Caribbean island where he grew up.

Mawuli grew up with his father, stepmother, and his siblings in the Islands as a family. He was a product of the public school system and graduated from one of the local high schools. He was considered an average student growing up. Despite his outward facade that appeared stable, he was troubled mentally, which stemmed from his childhood experiences.

Both Mawuli's biological parents had very similar personalities as young adults. Both parents could not see eye to eye as it related to raising Mawuli. They both had strong personalities. As a result, they separated while Mawuli was at a very young age. Not able to process and understand the dynamics of his life as a child, Mawuli became troubled by his upbringing. He did not know the reason for his parents' separation, but he knew that something was not right. He felt disconnected from everyone. Most of his relationships were broken.

His recollection of New York was very vague, but he distinctly remembered sitting at the window of his home, watching the neighborhood children play as they got wet from the fire hydrant. He remembered the closeness of the tall buildings and wide streets.

At around the age of five years old, he found himself living in the Islands. This was all new to him. Driving on this small Caribbean island was terrifying. He feared driving on roads surrounded by water. He thought to himself that he would probably have to live on a boat. He was relieved to find out he was actually living in a house and not in a boat.

Mawuli was blessed to have three parents. Each was individually special to him. Though they were young parents, raising a child was not a piece of cake. They both had to learn and grow as parents from their experiences. Mawuli was his father's first child and his mother's second. From his mom, he had a sister who was raised by his grandmother.

As the head of the household, his father was a good man who protected the family and ensured that there was food on the table. His father raised him with a very strict and rigid upbringing. Things had to go his way. His father was not open to letting him be free to express himself or even think for himself. Nor did he provide an opportunity for Mawuli to share his views on certain issues or even sit and talk or rationalize with him. Mawuli's father disciplined with the rod and strongly believed in physical discipline.

At a very young age, Mawuli had a special love for his grandmother, his father's mother. He often spent time at her home, where he could play with his cousins who were around the same age. He also had a step-grandmother, who assisted in raising him. After school, Mawuli was supposed to go by his step-grandmother's home as instructed by his father. Against his father's wishes, Mawuli would always go by his grandmother's, where he could play with his cousins. Each time, Mawuli would get such a beating from his father for not following his instructions that he can still remember the beatings as if they were yesterday.

As Mawuli grew, he wondered who his biological mother was and where she was. He often daydreamed that one day, she would show up by his school and say, "I am your mother." He thought about how tall she was, how she wore her hair, and how beautiful she was. Of all things, he wondered why she never came to look for him.

As a young boy and even as he grew to adulthood, he could not look his father in the eye without crying. He was often afraid to speak or answer a question incorrectly for fear of being beaten. This was the plantation / slave master mentality that was a part of him and of many of the elder Caribbean people growing up in the Islands. Unfortunately, this was the culture of the people and what they knew. The consistent beatings by his father and him not being able to express and be himself developed a fear and diminished his self-esteem. Not being able to think for himself made him unable to make sound and independent decisions. Combined with the absence of his biological mother in his life, Mawuli grew up unhappy and confused about life.

Mawuli expressed that while growing up, he never felt loved. He said he never recalled anyone telling him they loved him. He can only recall being hugged about once or twice while growing up. As a young teenager, he found himself gravitating to the so-called lowly of the society. He never felt a connection with his immediate family but felt it with his outside family of the weak, low self-esteemed hustlers, street people, freedom fighters, Rasta men, and the oppressed.

In the time when Mawuli was growing up in the Islands, the village raised the children, which meant that neighbors could correct or scold other neighbor's children without a problem. One evening, when he was about sixteen years old, he was in the neighborhood smoking marijuana. Someone in the neighborhood must have seen him and told his father. Mawuli distinctly remembers the story. He arrived at home to find his parents sitting, awaiting his arrival. His father asked him if he was smoking marijuana. Mawuli was high like a kite, and with smoke on his breath, he said no. Mawuli's father gave him a stern warning. His father told him that if he was ever caught smoking marijuana again, he would take off his belt and beat him regardless of where he was or who he was with. This made Mawuli furious as he had already built a reputation among his peers and could not have his father beating him in public. That was when Mawuli thought to himself it was time for him to leave his father's home. He had grown tired of the beatings. He often thought that if his father could only speak to him and reason with him, the relationship between them would have been much better. That very night, Mawuli packed a few of his personal items and ran away from home at the age of sixteen.

With no definitive plan and nowhere to go, Mawuli decided to go up in the hills on the western end of the island, not too far from his parents' home. There he managed to build up a shanty, and that was where he resided. In tenth grade, Mawuli stopped attending school. He stayed up in the hills during the day and roamed the streets of the small Caribbean island at night, keeping out of the sight of his parents.

Despite how he felt about his father's way of disciplining him, he never forgot the values his parents instilled in him. Strong values such as loyalty, family, church, and education, to name a few, were what he kept dear to his heart. After a few months of his new way of living, Mawuli decided that he wanted to return to high school. He had always had a liking for school and going to church. He voluntarily admitted himself into a juvenile center on the island for troubled youths with social and juvenile delinquency issues. At this center, he was able to get assistance with reenrollment in school in the tenth grade.

That summer, his grandmother took him to live with her. She lived in a small two-bedroom home, where she also housed some of his cousins and an uncle. For his grandmother, family was everything, and her home was open to her family and close friends.

Throughout his high school years, Mawuli cared and provided for himself. After school, he spent his time gambling and smoking marijuana. Before he entered the twelfth grade, Mawuli found himself back in the juvenile center. He was caught stealing plywood from the local college—plywood that he was going to use to build a more stable shanty. His time there was not easy, and he got in a physical altercation at the center where a young boy stabbed him in his back. The attending doctor told him that the knife almost pierced his heart. Nonetheless, that year, Mawuli entered the twelfth grade at his local high school. When he turned eighteen, he was released from the juvenile center, and he resided in the community housing projects on the western end of the island.

Mawuli continued his studies at the local high school where he studied carpentry as a trade. In the summers, he was afforded summer employment where he was hired to do carpentry. In 1976, Mawuli met the requirements for graduation. He was proud of his accomplishment and returned to his parents' home to give them an invitation to his graduation. That was his first time ever returning home after he ran away. Upon graduation, Mawuli received a scholarship to attend a trade school for carpentry. Unfortunately, with no ambition and goals set for himself, he allowed the scholarship to go to waste. Mawuli had the opportunity and skills to create a better life for himself, but due to his weak mind and inability to make independent and smart choices, he often settled for less.

While still living on the western end of the island with his grandmother, Mawuli's aunt shared with him that she knew someone who knew his biological mother. After several attempts to find this individual, Mawuli finally found the individual who gave him a phone number to contact his biological mother's mother—his grandmother. She resided on a sister island where Mawuli lived. After connecting with his grandmother, Mawuli got the contact number of his biological mother. He also learned that he was the only son and that he had three other sisters. After learning this information and connecting with his biological mother and siblings, he started to build a relationship with them over the phone since they resided off-island.

The opportunity to visit his grandmother and sister on the big sister island of where he resided presented itself for Mawuli. It was an absolute pleasure, and he was welcomed with open arms. This was his first time meeting them in person. His grandmother told him that from the time he entered the door, she knew that he was a part of the family.

Mawuli had fond memories of his grandmother, who lived to be over one hundred years old. He truly loved her.

With hopes of starting a new life for himself, Mawuli decided to travel to his birthplace, New York, to stay with his father's sister. Mawuli traveled on a one-way ticket. After a couple of weeks of staying with his aunt, she told him he could no longer stay at her home. With that being said, he reached out to his biological mother and explained his situation. His mother provided him with an address and told him to look for her at that location. This was a bit disheartening for Mawuli. He expected more from his biological mother. He did not know New York well enough to find his way around. He felt rejected by both his aunt and mother.

He took his belongings and went to live under a bridge between Bronx and Manhattan in New York. He lived there for about a month. There were times when Mawuli would go to Harlem to sleep. He would go to the top of the buildings with a cardboard box to sleep on. Sometimes, tenants would chase him; and other times, they would just let him rest. One time, while sleeping in an old truck, he awoke to find this giant man standing over him. The man stared at him for some time and walked way. It seemed as though he had a guardian angel watching over him.

During that time when he was homeless, he found a job as a glazier. The job required him to drive around the city repairing glass windows. In doing so, he ran into one of his father's bother, his uncle. Interestingly, he was in an area where a lot of Caribbean people migrated to in the '40s, '50s, and '60s. Mawuli's uncle gave him the contact number of another aunt who later took him in for about a month prior to him moving back to the Islands.

After his return to the Islands, he moved back to live with his grandmother on the western end of the Islands. He was employed as a maintenance worker at the Department of Education. He was responsible for repairs of the schools in his district. Though he was employed, he played softball and baseball for local government leagues;

however, he still lacked direction and purpose in his life. He hung out late nights on the corner in the housing community, gambled, and still associated with all segments of the community. He was introduced to the trade of mechanics by a guy in the community who had him work at his mechanic and body shop. To this date, he and the guy live as brothers.

Government Case

June of 1981 was the start of Mawuli B.'s tragic journey. He learned very soon how street life can lead to prison, death, or underachievement. On one cool Caribbean evening in June of 1981, as Mawuli walked on the sidewalk in his western community housing project, he was accosted by police dogs, armed police officers, and detectives. He was handcuffed and charged with murder in the first degree.

The murder charge stemmed from a murder that was committed earlier that month of June of 1981. A young man was shot to death on the eastern end of the island early in the morning, around 7:00 a.m. The premise of the government case was that on June 3, 1981, at approximately 7:00 a.m. on the eastern end of the island, Mawuli B. drove up to the victim, jumped out of a vehicle, and shot the victim multiple times, causing his death. It was said that he jumped back into the vehicle and drove off. The victim was shot in front of his housing community apartment building on the eastern end of the island. Mawuli's defense was that on the date of the murder, at approximately 7:00 a.m., he was on the western end of the island preparing to go to work and that he did not commit the murder, nor did he have any knowledge of the incident.

Mawuli was granted his constitutional right of a jury trial of his peers. He was appointed a first-time federal public defender from the US mainland, fresh out of law school. Mawuli's case was the first capital case of this young attorney's career.

On September of 1981, the trial began. Due to the high-profile nature of the case, it was difficult for the court to seat a jury panel of twelve jurors. As a result, the trial judge ordered his federal marshals to go to the streets to pull random people from around the island into the court to fill the jury pool. Thereafter, a jury panel was selected. Outside, the court was surrounded by armed federal agents for the entire trial proceedings.

The prosecution gave their opening remarks: Mawuli B., at approximately around 7:00 a.m. on June 3, 1981, on the east end of the island, drove up to the victim outside his housing community building and fatally shot the victim, and the jury must find him guilty. The defense attorney, federal public defender, gave his opening remarks as well: Mawuli B., at approximately around 7:00 a.m. on June 3, 1981, was on the western end of the island and could not have killed the victim, and the jury must find him innocent of all charges. As the trial unfolded, the government's star witness testified under oath. The prosecution depended heavily upon his testimony. He was known to the police and members of the community as a petite thief. He had run-ins with the law prior to his testimony. The government witness testified that at approximately 7:00 a.m. on June 3, 1981, he saw Mawuli B. jump out the vehicle with a mask over his face and shot and killed the victim. The government's star witness went on to testify that he saw Mawuli earlier that morning with the mask upon his face, and he saw his face.

This is the prosecuting attorney's line of questioning to the government's star witness:

> *Q. In June of 1981, did any police officer give you one hundred dollars?*
>
> *A. Yes.*
>
> *Q. Why?*
>
> *A. He gave it to me because I know him, so I asked for some money, and he gave me.*
>
> *Q. Did the police give you money to make a statement?*

A. No.
Q. Did the police give you money to testify?
A. No.
Q. Did anyone promise you anything?
A. No.

The government's star witness positively identified Mawuli sitting at the defense table at trial that day. After being questioned by the prosecution, the defense government's star witness was allowed to leave the stand.

To support the government's premise that Mawuli fired a gun on the morning of June 3, 1981, the prosecution called a local police officer to the witness stand. The direct examination is as follows:

Q. Please state your full name and where you are employed.
A. My name is Officer J., and I am employed by the Department of Public Safety.
Q. In what capacity?
A. I am a police officer assigned to the investigation—Bureau of Forensic Division.
Q. Now, on June 3, did you have occasions to administer a test on Mawuli B.?
A. I did.
Q. Where did . . . where and when did that took place?
A. It took place in the carpentry yard where he worked.
Q. What did you do to Mr. Mawuli B. at that time?
A. I administered an atomic absorption test, also known as a neutron activation test.
Q. Will you tell us how you administered the test?
A. I first advised Mr. Mawuli B. what I was going to do. I then broke the seal on the test and put on the sterile gloves provided in the kit. I then administered the nitrate solution on some sterile swabs, and I then proceeded to swab Mr. Mawuli's left hand palm, his left hand rear, his right hand

palm, and his right hand rear to include where the web area is located.

Q. Then after you administered the test, what, if anything, did you do with it?

A. I sealed the test and forwarded it.

The court: You did what?

The witness: Seal the test, put my initials on it, and forwarded it.

The court: Sealed the test?

The witness: Yes, the test package.

The court: I see.

Q. When you say packaged, what are those swabs contained in?

A. The swabs are placed in a sterile canister, which is in turn placed into a four-by-four plastic container. I then put the evidence seal on it, put my initials on it, and forwarded to the FBI office in Washington, DC.

The prosecution also called their expert witness from the FBI office in Washington, DC, to the stand.

A. My name is FBI Agent John D., and I am a special agent of the Federal Bureau of Investigation.

Q. How long have you been employed by the FBI?

A. I have been employed by the FBI since early 1978.

Q. In what capacity?

A. I am presently assigned to the Elemental Analysis Unit of the FBI laboratory in Washington, DC. In this capacity, I specialize in several methods of instrumental-chemical analysis. One such method is the one I used in this case—the neutron activation analysis.

Q. What is the purpose of this test?

A. In our laboratory, we use the tests to analyze swabs to determine the amount of barium and antimony on these swabs. The background of this is when a firearm is discharged, amounts of barium and antimony is found, which originated in the primer mix. Primer is that portion that sets off the explosion in the cartridge.

The witness: There was no cartridge case, but there was a cartridge case swab in Mr. Mawuli's kit.

The prosecution expert's witness went on to testify and told the jury that Mawuli's test was positive and that he fired a gun on the morning of June 3, 1981. The prosecution called other witnesses, including a witness who testified that he was Mawuli's cousin, but he failed to identify him while he was in front of him. The prosecution closed their case, and Mawuli presented his case.

Mawuli's witness was asked the following:

Q. Could you point him out here in court if you see him?
A. Yes.

The court: All right, walk out of the box and walk around anywhere you see the person named Mawuli and point to him (the witness complies).
The court: All right, he is pointing correctly to the defendant Mawuli.

Q. In the past, have you sold newspaper to Mawuli?
A. Yes, sometimes.
Q. And is he a neighbor of yours?
A. Yes.
Q. How far away from you does he live?
A. Across the street.
Q. Did you sell him a newspaper on the morning of June 3, 1981?

A. Yes.

Q. Where did you sell him the paper?

A. At his house.

Q. Did you see him when you sold him the paper?

A. Yes, yes.

Q. Do you recall what time this was?

A. Seven fifteen to seven twenty.

Mawuli's defense called more witnesses to support his defense that he was on the western end of the island when the alleged crime was committed. The evidence from both sides were submitted to the jury for deliberation after closing remarks from the prosecution and Mawuli's defense counsel.

The Tragic Journey

On September 27, 1981, a few minutes after 4:00 p.m. that Sunday, a nervous jury group of ten women and two men returned a guilty verdict against Mawuli. After a total of six and a half hours of deliberation on Saturday evening and Sunday afternoon in the Islands, the twelve jurors came into the courtroom at 4:10 p.m. Their faces were twisted, and staring straight ahead with hands trembling, the foreman slowly rose to give the verdict. The other jurors, all with strained faces and some fidgeting with their hands, continued to stare straight ahead. Some gave brief side-glances at the table where Mawuli sat. As Mawuli stood there, he could not believe the verdict as it was read.

More than half of the courtroom spectators, seemingly angry and disappointed with the verdict, hastily left the courtroom. Ten US marshals standing behind Mawuli's defense table and four at the door in the back of the courtroom remained alert as people left. Officers lined the third-floor balcony and the lower floors of the US courtroom.

On September 28, 1981, Mawuli's birthday, he was sentenced to spend the rest of his natural life in prison. He was twenty-four years of age on the day he was sentenced to natural life imprisonment.

Journey of Imprisonment

During Mawuli's first ten years of wrongful imprisonment, he was angry and mad. He was mad with the world and everyone in it. During those years, he went through so much mentally and emotionally; not knowing when he will be released put so much stress on him. If he even had a release date, though it may have been many years, at least he had a date to look forward to. Mawuli expressed that not knowing when he will ever be released was the hardest part of a life sentence.

From June of 1981 to December of 1981, Mawuli was housed in the islands at Fort Christian jail, which was built in 1671. This jail was once a fort where slaves were kept back in the day. There were no toilets or sinks in the cell. There were never less than four inmates at a time in the cell with one bunk bed.

By January of 1982, Mawuli was relocated to the big island of Saint Croix in the Bureau of Corrections (GGACF). GGACF was a prison for sentenced inmates, while Saint Thomas Fort Christian was mainly for pretrial housing. GGACF had programs like GED and computer classes, work programs, and arts and craft programs. GGACF had a yard that was open in the morning, when cells were open, and the yard was closed around 7:00 p.m. Cells were locked down at 8:00 p.m. Cells there were a little more modern with toilets and sinks. They were also furnished with a mattress on a concrete slab. It was a shocking blow when the Third Circuit Court of Appeals affirmed his 1981 conviction and denied his appeal in January of 1983. Prior to that opinion, Mawuli was confident that the judicial system worked and that his wrongful conviction would be reversed.

In March of 1983, Mawuli was again relocated to the Federal Bureau of Prisons in Oxford, Wisconsin. He distinctly remembers the night when two prison guards opened the cell door and said, "Let's go. We're taking you to the mainland." They placed handcuffs on him and took him to another facility called Anna's Hope for the night. He was not allowed to take any of his property, only the clothes he wore. Anna's Hope was a few miles away from GGACF. The following morning, he was allowed one phone call. He called his parents on Saint Thomas and told them he was being shipped out to the mainland, and he did not know where he was being transferred to. The very minute he hung up the phone, he was chained around his waist. He was then put on a commercial flight out of Saint Croix's airport to the mainland.

Mawuli landed in Madison, Wisconsin. The weather was extremely cold. He felt like he was in an icebox. His body was shivering, and his teeth chattered beyond his control. They arrived at night, so he slept at a county jail in Madison. After a few days there, they traveled miles to the Federal Correction Institution at Oxford, Wisconsin. It was a culture shock and new experience for him. For the first time in his life, he saw a Native American homosexual. He never knew there were Native American homosexuals. Prior to the experience, he only saw how Native Americans were portrayed on television, and they were usually warriors. He quickly learned that homosexuals are of different cultures and races.

He experienced so many different cultures, nationalities, belief systems, etc. He met members of the Aryan Brotherhood, Black Panther, Mafia figures, Native American freedom fighters, Puerto Rican freedom fighters, Fountain Valley Brothers, Crips leaders, Bloods leaders, drug dealers, terrorists, cold killers, etc. He sat with, ate with, and worked with all these men. He did not stay long at Oxford. After nine months, a correctional officer got killed when he was there. Thereafter, busloads of prisoners were shipped out, and he was one of those inmates shipped out. Prior to that incident where the correction officer got killed, he was in solitary confinement for having a knife in the cell, along with his cellmate.

Mawuli again was relocated to FCI Terre Haute in Indiana. His experiences continued to unfold. He fasted for the first time with the Muslim community. The occasion was Ramadan. At Terre Haute, he got exposed to the weight room. Prisoners from his hometown in the Islands who were also incarcerated at Terre Haute were into exercising. He later got into it as well. In every prison he traveled to, he would first seek out the Virgin Islands' prisoners at the institution. Most of the island prisoners knew Mawuli or knew of him and his unfortunate situation. It was always a positive reunion meeting his island comrades at the prison he stayed at. Once again, Mawuli got into trouble at Terre Haute prison. Correctional officers at the facility found a homemade knife in his cell. Thereafter, he was relocated to FCI Oklahoma in Oklahoma City. Oklahoma City's prison was an older facility and housed high-security inmates. Summers were extremely hot, and winters were very cold at FCI Oklahoma.

FCI Oklahoma provided even more experiences for him. One of his biggest experiences there came with one of his island homeboys. One day, his homeboy from the Islands pointed to a young prisoner from Washington, DC, and told him the guy was his boy. Mawuli was in shock. He responded in his island dialect, "Wha? Wha you mean your boi?" His homeboy replied that the guy was his girl. What was so alarming to Mawuli was that the DC guy's girlfriend and children used to travel to Oklahoma to visit him.

At times, it was difficult not to get in trouble. In 1984, he got into trouble once again. While at Oklahoma City, a well-known dreadlocked American homosexual pushed him over a broom in the kitchen. He was in the kitchen sweeping. In the federal prison system, everyone had to work. The guy said the broom was his. Mawuli watched him and then threw the broom to the floor. The guy then stepped toward Mawuli and pushed him. He was too big and strong for Mawuli to fistfight with. Later that day, he went for a homemade knife and stabbed him in the shoulder. He thanked God he survived because this would have been more trouble for him. Thereafter, he was shipped to the United States Penitentiary of Lompoc, California.

He found himself in USP Lompoc, California, in 1985 after a long bus ride from Oklahoma City. During that long trip, they had some holdover stops between Oklahoma and California. At one of the holdover stops, the inmates were ordered to get naked. Then they were hosed down by correctional officers with insect spray, just like a cattle. On another holdover stop at a county jail, the jail was so dirty, overcrowded, and nasty that he wanted to bawl like a child. He spent one holiday season at the FCI La Tuna since all buses were on hold for the holidays. There he got the news that one of the Fountain Valley prisoners from the Islands hijacked a plane to Cuba while being shipped from the Islands to the mainland. When he got to USP Lompoc, he met two elder Islands prisoners. Both played a big role in molding Mawuli into a mature man. They inspired him to pursue a college education while locked up and to focus on obtaining his freedom. They sat him down and advised him not to keep knives and weapons in his possession and that he must focus on one day becoming free. This was the best advice they shared with Mawuli that one day paid off.

His arrival at USP Lompoc found him still angry for being incarcerated over a murder he did not commit. However, it was there that he got a glimmer of hope for the better. He began taking classes in the psychology department that helped him to deal with his anger and other psychological issues. At USP Lompoc, instructors from Chapman University in Orange County, California, came to the prison to teach college courses. Mawuli later obtained an associate of arts degree and a bachelor of arts degree in social psychology from USP Lompoc's education program.

Overall, he spent twelve years at USP Lompoc. All those years, he focused on his freedom from his wrongful imprisonment and becoming a better person and improving his skills. Over those years, there were times he felt so depressed with his life sentence hanging over his head. In spite of this, he had faith that one day, he would be freed. It was still depressing serving time at times. Over the years of his incarceration, there were experiences of riots, prison murders, fights, and many appeals being denied. Once, there was a riot between the Crips and Bloods during a program where he was the master of ceremonies.

On one occasion at USP Lompoc, a prison guard got murdered, and the prison was locked down for one month. On the first two weeks, the inmates were fed bag lunches for breakfast, lunch, and dinner. The food was not filling that Mawuli became so weak and fainted, hitting his head against the sink in the cell. He had to seek medical attention. Things were getting crazy while he was at USP Lompoc. Two VI prisoners also got murdered. Things were rough, and the food was of low quality. It was common to find things like roaches or metal particles in your food. With no other option, Mawuli would just put them on the side and eat the meal provided.

To cope with the depressive and down moments, Mawuli would utilize various programs at the institution. The arts and crafts program was one of those programs that were therapeutic for him. Another was the chaplain services. He would go there to listen to Bob Marley music, which was uplifting. Also, he attended different religious services. The psychology department program was extremely helpful too in uplifting his spirit. All these programs assisted in carrying him through the depressing moments of his wrongful imprisonment.

His family, friends, loved ones, and faith in God helped to carry him through those hard times of his wrongful imprisonment as well. The letters, cards, phone calls, and visits received during that time were priceless. He was grateful for all those who didn't give up on him or turn their backs on him, especially when he wanted to give up on himself. There were new people he met while he was incarcerated, and they visited and treated him as though they knew him from the Islands. He thanked God for them all.

After eleven years at USP Lompoc, he requested a transfer to USP Allenwood in Pennsylvania. Allenwood was a new penitentiary, but all the cells were double bunk (two beds in a cell). At USP Lompoc, he bunked in a single cell most of his time there. For three months at USP Lompoc, he bunked in a double cell with another inmate. This was the first time he saw someone shoot drugs into their veins. His cellmate was a drug addict.

USP Allenwood was a different type of penitentiary from USP Lompoc. At USP Allenwood, he experienced being under the night sky with stars, something he hadn't experienced in eleven years. Every evening, he would go out under the stars until the yard closed at 9:00 p.m. At USP Allenwood, he also received visits from family and friends since it was close to New York. It was there where he met his biological mother for the first time since he was four years of age. At that visit, he was about thirty-five years old. After a few months at USP Allenwood, he was surprisingly shipped back to USP Lompoc. The administration never told him the reason for the transfer.

Once back at Lompoc, he fell right back into the routine. After one year, he was ready to leave USP Lompoc. After that year, he requested to be transferred to USP Beaumont in Texas. USP Beaumont in Texas was a newly built prison. However, prisoners needing discipline from all over the federal prison system were sent there. Mawuli just wanted to get out of USP Lompoc, and USP Beaumont was the only prison he was allowed to go to at that time. USP Beaumont had a gun tower in the center of its yard. Whenever there was a fight or stabbing, they fired one shot, and you had better lay on the ground or be subjected to be shot at.

Mawuli had no problems and learned early in his penitentiary journey to respect everyone and to stay away from gambling, homosexual activity, and drugs. This would help to avoid problems in prison. He enrolled in a one-year psychology program at USP Beaumont that offered anger management classes. After completing that program, he was granted a transfer to a lower-level institution, the Federal Correctional Institution of Coleman in Florida (FCI), after spending fourteen years in high-security prisons.

FCI Coleman was fairly new and overcrowded. It was a step down in security from the high-level penitentiaries. There was less violence at FCI. Over half of its population were government informants. As a result, there was nothing that went on in FCI that the administrators didn't know. Once, a candy machine was broken into in the morning. By afternoon, they found out who broke into the machine. The population was young, and over half of the inmates had drug-related cases.

Due to the Islands' financial crisis, the government was forced to remove all the island prisoners from the federal prison system. The government had a contract agreement with the federal government to house island prisoners in its prisons. Since the government was unable to pay the federal government, they returned all its prisoners, except for a few that they contracted to privately house in state prisons in America. Mawuli was fortunate to be one of those prisoners who were returned to the Bureau of Corrections, where he initially began his sentence.

In December of 2000, Mawuli was transshipped from FCI Coleman in Florida to USP Atlanta and was held over there. Standing in that windy and cold airport platform wearing a thin orange jumpsuit and blue karate shoes while the prison guards walked around in their thick winter coats and big boots was no joke. He couldn't wait to get back to the Islands.

The next day, Mawuli was sent to the Federal Transfer Center in Oklahoma City. The transit center was located in the Oklahoma City airport. The planes would taxi right up to the terminal spot where the inmates walked from the plane straight into the transit terminal. The federal prison buses would also drive straight into the building. The building held men and women and was about six stories. The hallways would be filled with long lines of men and women chained from waist to foot. The lines consisted of all ages, all races, and all nationalities. As the inmates got to the end of the line, they would have to climb up on a wooden box where officers would take off their foot chains and waist chains. Then they were led into a room for medical review before they were sent to their holdover unit. When they left, they had to go through the same procedure. It reminded Mawuli of those picture s of slaves chained up heading into those slave ships. Many of the VI prisoners from all across the federal prison systems met up at the Federal Oklahoma Transit Center. It was a family reunion. It was great seeing people, especially those you did not see in years, and it was an opportunity to build relationships with those you just met.

In a couple of days, the inmates were transshipped from Oklahoma City Federal Transit Center to Puerto Rico. When Mawuli got to Puerto Rico, he just knew he was home from the interaction between the island prison guards and island inmates. Some inmates went straight to Saint Croix. Mawuli was in the group that was held over until the next day and then transshipped from Puerto Rico to Saint Croix Bureau of Corrections. He arrived in Saint Croix on December 15, 2000. He was housed at the Golden Grove Correctional Facility (GGACF).

GGACF was an old institution by the time he returned to the Islands. There were at least six returning from the mainland prison system. GGACF was not the same as when he left in 1983. In those days, there were single cells. On his return in 2000, all cells were double. The population was filled with younger prisoners. There were little structures. It took a while for him to adjust to his new environment. CD players were new to him, as well as cell phones.

GGACF afforded him the opportunity to effectively pursue his quest to obtain justice from his wrongful imprisonment. He got assigned a job in the business office. This job allowed him to travel through the institution and interact with the staff, administrators, and all prisoners. He got into the GGACF arts and crafts program, which afforded him the great opportunity to go into the free community with a correctional officer. This program allowed him to travel to Saint Thomas.

In 2004, he participated in the Carnival Food Fair, where he and other inmates sold handmade arts and crafts. Mawuli was granted the opportunity to travel to schools to share his experience with local students. GGACF helped Mawuli to reconnect with his community and especially the youths of the Islands.

Truth Conquers Falsehood

Five years into Mawuli B.'s wrongful imprisonment, an evidentiary hearing was held in the district court of the Islands. This 1985 evidentiary hearing was based on an affidavit from the government's star witness that says he lied under oath at Mawuli's trial. At the evidentiary hearing, the government's star witness testified that he was forced to recant his trial testimony. He further testified at the hearing that his trial testimony was true.

Newly discovered evidence was introduced at this evidentiary hearing, and two witnesses testified under oath at the hearing that the government's star witness was asleep at the time of the alleged crime.

The court: *Very good, call whatever witnesses you want.*
Attorney: *Your Honor, may I proceed?*
Witness: *Q. Do you know the government's star witness?*
A. Yes, I do.
Q. How long have you known him?
A. Well, eight years.
Q. Do you remember the evening before that morning?
A. Yes.
Q. Do you remember if the government's star witness was in your apartment?
A. He comes around. Zarro comes around at nine o'clock.
Q. Zarro?

A. Came around at nine o'clock.

The court: Who is Zarro?

Witness: NJ.

Q. Is that the girlfriend of the government's star witness at that time?

A. Yes.

Q. You remembered the morning when the victim was killed?

A. Yes.

Q. Could you tell the court what you remembered?

The court: About what?

Attorney: About the morning?

The court: No, that question is too general, and I won't permit it.

Q. Could you tell the court where you were and what you heard that morning?

The court: I will interpose. That's totally irrelevant.

Q. Did you hear shots that morning?

A. Yes.

Q. You heard shots, and who were you with when you heard the shots?

The court: Excuse me. Don't answer the question.

Q. Could you tell the judge you heard shots that morning?

A. Yes.

Q. Was anyone sleeping in your living room?

A. The government's star witness and NJ.

Q. NJ is that Zarro, his girlfriend?

A. Yes.

Q. Where were you sleeping in your living room?

A. On a bed couch in the living room.

Q. This is at the time you heard the shots?

A. While they were sleeping.

Q. Yes, thank you. When they were sleeping, is that when you heard the shots?

A. Yes.

Q. You woke NJ.

A. Yes.

Q. And the government's star witness was sleeping?

A. Yes.

Q. And then what happened after that?

A. Then NJ came into the kitchen to look for some sugar, but it didn't have no more. She woke up the government's star witness, and they both left and went down the road to see the shooting.

Q. Did any police interview you?

A. No.

Attorney: Q. Good morning, miss, could you please state your name.

A. NJ.

Q. Are you known as NJ?

A. No.

Q. Does anyone call you NW?

A. No.

Q. Do you know the government's star witness?

A. Yes.

Q. Have you ever been his girlfriend?

A. Yes.

Q. The morning that the victim was shot, where were you?

A. At R.'s house, sleeping.

Q. At R.'s house, sleeping?

A. Yes.

Q. With whom were you sleeping?

A. With the government's star witness.

Q. And who woke you up?

A. R.

Q. What did you do when you awoke?

A. Well, she woke me up and told me there was something going on down there.

Q. What was that something?

A. Well, it was the killing of the victim, and I woke up the government's star witness, but he was still sleeping. I woke him up again and told him that something was going on down there, and he looked through the window. After a little while, we went down.

A. No.

Q. You did go to the prosecutor's office with the government's star witness on more than one occasion, isn't that correct?

A. Yes.

Q. And you were never asked any questions at any time?

A. No.

At the evidentiary hearing, the government's star witness testified:

Q. You were shown pictures of people you know as Mawuli B., right?

A. Yes.

Q. That was down in the prosecutor's office?

A. Yes.

The government's star witness further testified:

Q. You got money for a ticket right after the trial?

A. Yes.

Q. And you left here and went to the States?

A. I went to the States.

Q. Other than that money, did you get anything else?

A. Yes.

Q. What else did you get?

A. $600 more.

Q. $600?

A. Yes.

Q. Who gave you $600?

A. The prosecutor sent it to me.

Q. Were you told by the prosecutor or by anybody else that they would pay you to testify?

A. No.

Q. You were in Texas. So you did not get the money here? You were already in Texas?

A. No. I got $600 here, and they sent me $600 more.

Q. So that's $1,200?

A. That's $1,200.

At the end of the evidentiary hearing, September 18, 1985, the trial judge handed down his opinion. He ruled that the recantation affidavit of the government's star witness was forced and coerced; therefore, the conviction would stand. He also stated in his opinion that he would not consider the newly discovered evidence at proceeding and that it would have to be addressed at another proceeding.

As Mawuli pursued to prove his innocence years after the evidentiary hearing, Mawuli obtained additional newly discovered evidence that the government's star witness was paid by the police for confidential information in the victim's homicide. On September 25, 1981, at 10:05 a.m., the government's star witness received from a detective through the investigation bureau of the Department of Public Safety the following item: the sum of $750 for confidential information in the victim homicide, witnessed by the detective and signed by the government's star witness.

Mawuli continued to prove his innocence even after his release. In 2016, he revisited his trial records with more knowledge about the atomic absorption test, also known as the neutron activation test. This test was used by detectives to prove that Mawuli fired a firearm on the morning of June 3, 1981, which he denied. The FBI stated that his results of the test were the highest they had ever found from a test. This was puzzling to Mawuli, so he did his own research on the subject since he contested that he had never fired a firearm that day and had nothing to do with the homicide. With new knowledge on neutron activation testing, Mawuli revisited his trial records to identify new findings by the FBI in Washington, DC.

The trial records revealed the following:

> *Q. What did you do to Mawuli at the time?*
> *A. I administered an atomic absorption test, also known as a neutron activation test.*
> *Q. Then after you administered the test, what, if anything, did you do with it?*
> *A. I sealed the test and forwarded it.*
> *The court:*
> *Q. You sealed the test?*
> *A. Yes, the test package.*

The trial records go on to reveal the following:

FBI agent: (Stated his name for the court and stated that he is employed as a special agent with the Federal Bureau of Investigations.)

> *Q. In what capacity?*
> *A. I am presently assigned to the element analysis unit of the FBI in Washington, DC.*

The witness: There was no cartridge case, but there was a cartridge case swab included in Mawuli's kit.

The trial records showed inconsistencies. According to the VI police officers, they sealed Mawuli's swab kit after administering the test. The FBI found Mawuli's swab kit (that was supposed to sealed) with a gun cartridge swab inside his hand swab kit. Evidently, the swab kit of Mawuli B. was contaminated by the enclosed gun cartridge swab. This proved that the findings were inaccurate.

The Jury Found Him Guilty

This was a case where one man was alleged to be at two places at one time. Mawuli stated that on June 3, 1981, he was on the west end of the Caribbean island around 7:00 a.m., the time the alleged crime took place. The prosecution alleged that Mawuli was on the eastern end of the Caribbean island, where they claimed he shot and killed the victim. Mawuli presented evidence that he was on the western end of the island at the time of the crime.

The prosecution submitted to the jury evidence from their star witness who was asleep at the time of the alleged crime. The jury found Mawuli guilty based on perjury. The appointed attorney of Mawuli's trial was ineffective. He failed to interview witnesses and investigate prior to the trial. The ineffectiveness of Mawuli's attorney allowed for the prosecution's star witness, who was asleep during the alleged crime, to testify that he was seen at the crime scene. The prosecution's unethical practices contributed to Mawuli's wrongful imprisonment.

The government's star witness testified at the evidentiary hearing that he met with the prosecution in their office without legal representation to view pictures of Mawuli. The prosecution failed to disclose favorable evidence to the defense during the trial. The government's star witness testified that he was not paid or promised any money in connection with the case. However, the prosecution testified that the star witness received money to purchase a plane ticket and $750 in exchange for confidential information. He was later paid $600 on two different occasions.

Evidence that the star witness received money in connection with the case and in exchange for information was pertinent information in the defense of Mawuli's case. Had this information been presented initially, the outcome of the case might have been different. The prosecution's submission of evidence that had been tampered with played a role in his wrongful conviction. Had the proper procedures been followed in securing Mawuli's swab kit, then the evidence would not have been contaminated. If the jury was presented with accurate information and specific pertinent information relative to the case was not withheld, then Mawuli's chance of having a fair trial would have been upheld. After his wrongful conviction, Mawuli continued to fight to prove his innocence. The newly disclosed evidence proved that Mawuli did not have a fair trial. Despite his wrongful imprisonment, Mawuli was given an opportunity of a lifetime—a second chance to freedom.

Free at Last

It was in 2006, the former governor's final year in office, when word was out that he was planning to commute and/or pardon prisoners of the Islands who were imprisoned with long sentences. Mawuli's strategy was to submit all evidence of his innocence, along with an executive petition to the governor. He submitted documents of his degrees and prison achievements over those twenty-five years of his wrongful imprisonment. Additionally, he submitted evidence of the perjury by the government's star witness and provided proof of how the evidence presented by the government was tampered with.

As the year 2006 came to a close, there was extreme anxiety and stress among the prisoners at GGACF. Everyone was praying and hoping that they would be one of those prisoners the governor would grant relief from the long years of imprisonment. It was the morning of January 2, 2007, that Mawuli made a phone call to his aunt on Saint Croix. She was the first to let him know he was one of the prisoners who were granted relief. He distinctly recalls the exact words used over the phone: "Nephew, your papers were signed by the governor for your release." No words could express the relief, joy, and happiness that good news brought to his life. She went on to tell him, "Don't tell anyone as yet. The news was not officially released."

Mawuli could not hold in the good news. He wanted to share the news of joy with someone. As his aunt hung up the phone, he called an organization in New Jersey that helps the wrongfully imprisoned seek justice. This organization had been supporting Mawuli throughout his journey, providing inspiration, guidance, and knowledge for many years during his imprisonment. He called a representative from the organization who had helped him during his journey. As he began to share with her the good news, he broke down in tears over the phone. He was lost for words; he just wept until he hung up the phone. As he tried to contain himself, he tried calling a good friend in California who did time with him while housed in USP Lompoc. Once again, as he began telling him the good news of freedom, he broke down in tears and began weeping like a child. He didn't know how to handle the news. He had to go for a walk in the prison yard.

Later that day, the local evening news on television made the announcement. The local news read the list of names of the men and women whom the governor pardoned and whose sentences had been commuted during his last term as governor of the Virgin Islands. His name was on the top of the list. It was a joyous evening for a few and a sad evening for so many with long sentences whose names were not called. That night, after the prison guards locked the gate of Mawuli's cell for the last time, he went on his knees in tears and thanked God for having mercy upon him and for touching the governor's heart, moving him to grant him relief after years of wrongful imprisonment. On his knees, he wept and wept as he thanked God for freedom at last. It felt like a heavy weight was lifted off his shoulder and spirit. The emotion of happiness covered him at the same time.

It was a blessing from God Almighty to obtain freedom after years of Mawuli's fighting and being rejected, denied, and subjected to some of the most dehumanizing treatment there is. Serving a mandatory life-without-parole sentence for a crime that one did not do can cause mental as well as physical breakdown. He was indeed blessed to be freed.

The morning of January 3, 2007, Mawuli woke up bright and early. He brought some of his close prison friends to his cell. He instructed them to take anything they wanted from the cell—things like books, pens, pencils, etc. It was amazing how fast that cell was cleaned out.

There was one close friend whom Mawuli held close to his heart. This man is still serving a life-without-parole sentence. They both looked each other in the eyes. Mawuli could see his happiness for him, but at the same time, he could feel and see the sadness as he was not leaving with him. He will never forget that moment.

That evening, Mawuli signed some release papers and then exited the R & D door unto the street of freedom after twenty-five years of wrongful imprisonment. About five other men were released by executive order. Mawuli and the men held hands and prayed together, thanking the Almighty and praying for continued guidance. One of the family members of one of the other freed men put one hundred dollars in Mawuli's hand. Mawuli's aunt came to pick him up. That was a blissful day. He called family and friends to share his news of freedom. They couldn't believe he was finally freed. From the first day of his imprisonment, Mawuli always felt in his heart that he would be freed, but he never thought it would have taken twenty-five years.

Gratitude and Forgiveness

Mawuli extends his sincerest gratitude to his mother for raising him with love. He wishes to thank her for being by his side throughout his journey. As he reflects on his childhood, he feels sincere remorse for the pain and hurt he may have caused over the years and expresses his unconditional love for her.

He also expresses a heartfelt thank-you to his biological mother, for without her, he will not be here on earth today. He wishes to thank and acknowledge her many prayers and love over the years. He asks for her forgiveness for the thoughts he had bottled inside without knowing the full story.

He acknowledges his late grandmother who showed her unconditional love and support for him during the course of her life. Although she is not with him today, he pleads for her forgiveness for the trials he put her through and knows in his heart that if she was here today, she would have forgiven him and would have been proud of his victory and accomplishments. She forever holds a special place in his heart.

He extends his special thanks to one of his former girlfriends for loving him when he didn't love himself. He asks for her forgiveness for the pain and hurt he caused in her life, and to this day, he still has love for her.

To his father, who has been a strong support for him and his family, he wishes to say thank you from the bottom of his heart. He asks for forgiveness for the hurt and stress he may have caused. He expresses love and appreciation for his father.

To his family, supporters, and fellow inmates who have supported, prayed, wrote letters on his behalf, and assisted in any way—no matter how big or small—during his journey, he expresses his sincere appreciation. He cannot say thank you enough. Without his faith and God by his side, he could not have gotten through this tragic ordeal. He gives God Almighty all the praises for his grace, guidance, protection, and willpower to get over his many challenges and for healing him and allowing him to forgive and love himself and others.

Prison life can be hell on earth; however, God used Mawuli B.'s wrongful imprisonment to help him and others. It helped him to find himself, to truly get to know himself, and to love himself. All those years locked up in a prison cell with only God by his side forced him to do some soul-searching. The opportunity to participate in some of the spiritual and psychological programs he attended while in prison helped to define his character and made him a better person. He overcame his bitterness, anger, lack of purpose, and low self-esteem.

Some Experiences after His Release

- The first food he had eaten was a veggie pizza.
- One of his first activities took place on the island of Saint Croix. He participated in the Crucian Festival J'ouvert and was jumping up and "wuking" up.
- He experienced his first tub bath and did not know how to operate the faucet. He literally had to call for assistance.
- On his first time traveling after his release, he packed his clothes in two large brown paper bags after learning that people no longer travel with paper bags but luggage or suitcases.
- After being confined for so many years, his sense of direction was distorted that he often had problems with direction. He would get lost in stores and would not know the difference between north and south or east and west.
- He was not accustomed to being out after a certain time. Once it got dark, he would feel very uncomfortable and would need to go home. He was still institutionalized.
- At his first employment after incarceration, the employees on the job protested. They didn't want to work among a convict of murder. He was transferred to a different department.
- He was denied government assistance.
- Days after his release, he broke down in tears. He felt so helpless in this new world. He was dependent upon others to get around

and adapt to this new society. Talking to family helped him get over his ordeal. He relied heavily on his faith in God.

- So accustomed to not having options, when asked by his brother what he wanted, he was lost for words. For years, he never had the choice to choose what he wanted to eat or have.
- Overall, he received lots of love and support from his family, his friends, and his community. People prayed for him and read about his plight in the local newspaper. People learned of his situation over the WSTA radio station. He expressed his love and appreciation.

Lessons Learned

- There is a force, spirit, energy, and God that is greater than man. No matter what we call this force, spirit, energy, or your God, this is what will carry you through your trials and tribulations.
- You have to believe, work hard, and never give up on your goals and dreams.
- Get your education and gain knowledge, especially in the areas in your life you enjoy doing.
- Family is sometimes all you have through your life's trials and tribulations. Love them, forgive them, and embrace them.
- Don't be quick to judge. Sometimes, things are not what they seem to be.
- You must have inner strength to say no to drugs, guns, and all negative things that will steal your future and your joy.
- Remember, all our actions and decisions have consequences, whether good or bad. Our choices have consequences.
- Think, think before you make a decision, especially if it involves negativity. Always think before you act.
- If we find ourselves with anger or a bad temper, we should seek professional help. These emotions can cause you to make bad decisions that can destroy your life and others.
- A friend will never lead you astray. A friend will give his or her life for you. A friend will tell you the truth even if it hurts. A friend accepts you the way you are.

- Be yourself. No two people are the same, so be proud of being unique. Be you and love you. Love and accept everything about who you are.
- Learn from your mistakes. We all make mistakes in this life. However, learn from your mistakes so that you can become wiser, more mature, and become a better person.
- Never give up. Life is a journey. Some of the hills we'd have to climb involve injustice, pain, disappointment, hurt, etc. We have to be steadfast, faithful, and resilient. Victory will be the reward.
- You can't make a person do something they don't want to do. All you can do is share your knowledge and wisdom with a person. They will have to be the one to make their own decisions.
- Listen to others' wisdom and experiences. The biggest man was once a child. Through living, a person gains experiences and wisdom. Their wisdom and experiences can help us in making good and positive decisions in our lives.
- Always think highly of yourself. Think highly of yourself despite what you have been through. Remember, no one is better than you. We all were created in God's image. You are the best.
- Own up to your actions. Be a big person and own up to your actions.
- Every day, you can learn something. No matter how smart you are, there are things you don't know. No one knows everything. Each day is an opportunity to learn something new.
- A man is known by the company he keeps. If you associate yourself with bankers and carry yourself like a banker, people will think you're a banker even though you might not be. In the same way, if you associate yourself with gangsters and carry yourself as one, people will think you're a gangster even if you're not.
- You were born for a purpose. You were not born to waste your life locked up in prison. You have a great purpose. Live and reach into yourself for it.

- You can't please everyone. No matter what you do or say, someone will not be in agreement. Just be true to yourself and do what your heart tells you is right.
- Each of us has the power to choose good or bad. It is our right. No matter what our peeps do or decide, it doesn't matter to us because we have our own mind to choose. Let's choose positively and make the right choices.
- People do change. Yes, people do change. When you change the way you think, then your behavior changes. A man is what he thinks.
- Be a leader. Don't let others dictate your life.
- Apply conflict resolution when facing conflicts.
- It is easy to fall in prison but very difficult to get out, even for those innocently imprisoned.
- Drugs, crimes, and violence can lead you into the trap of imprisonment, an unproductive life, and an unfulfilled life. Avoid the trap.
- Respect and manners will carry you far.

These are just some of the many lessons Mawuli had learned from his wrongful imprisonment and life experiences. Over the years, he had shared these lessons with students, individuals from juvenile programs, etc. in the hope that his life lessons could touch their lives in a positive way.

Favorite Biblical Passages

Psalm 142
I cried unto the LORD with my voice; with my voice
unto the LORD did I make my supplication.

[2] I poured out my complaint before him; I
shewed before him my trouble.
[3] When my spirit was overwhelmed within me, then thou knewest my
path. In the way wherein [walked have they privily laid a snare for me.
[4] I looked on my right hand, and beheld, but there was no man that
would know me: refuge failed me; no man cared for my soul.
[5] I cried unto thee, O LORD: I said, Thou art my
refuge and my portion in the land of the living.
[6] Attend unto my cry; for I am brought very low: deliver
me from my persecutors; for they are stronger than I.
[7] Bring my soul out of prison, that I may praise
thy name: the righteous shall compass me about;
for thou shalt deal bountifully with me.

Quotes of Freedom

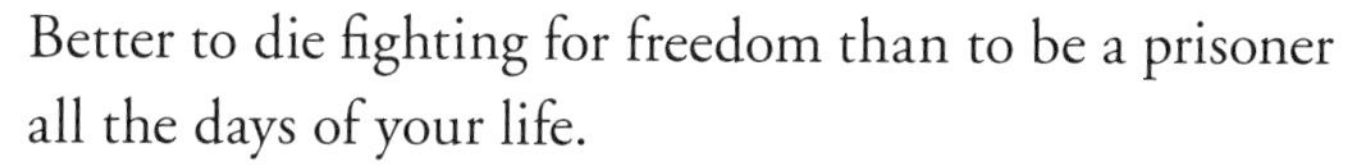

Better to die fighting for freedom than to be a prisoner all the days of your life.

—Bob Marley

For to be free is not merely to cast off one's chains, but to live in a way that respects and enhances the freedom of others.

—Nelson Mandela

Freedom is being you without anyone's permission.

—Anonymous

The journey and tribulations of Mawuli's life—both negative and positive—have made him the man he is today. He uses his life experiences to aid in making sound decisions in his life. His story is an inspiration to many and continues to impact the lives of those he comes in contact with, particularly the youths. Without a doubt, Mawuli can truly say that he is *blessed to be free.*

Blessed to Be Free Captured Moments

All photos were taken by Keith Benjamin.

Winter in New York City

Saint Thomas, USVI

Saint Thomas, USVI

Saint Thomas, USVI

Yellow cedar (*Tecoma stans*), national flower of the VI

Beautiful sunset in Saint Thomas, USVI

Crystal clear seawater of the VI

Carnival cultural event,
Saint Thomas, UVI

Made in the USA
Middletown, DE
22 June 2019

In my preparation for this memoir, I have had several discussions with and heard from innocent men and women of how clear evidence were presented to the courts and their motions for release on the grounds of their innocence were denied by the courts. Some of these individuals served time and were released after years, in spite of evidence of their innocence. There were some who were blessed to be free by a parole board and some by way of executive relief. In the case of release of the parole board or executive relief, the innocent individual retained prison records. Though these individuals may be innocent, in the eyes of society, they are still considered guilty because of the prison records hanging over their heads.

I often wonder why is it so hard to obtain freedom from a wrongful conviction, particularly when the evidence of innocence is before the courts. Perhaps it is hard for people to admit their wrongdoing regardless of the negative impact on one's life.

This memoir talks about a man, Mawuli B., who presented facts and evidence of his innocence to the courts, but his motion for release was denied for years. After the review of Mr. Mawuli B's case by the executive branch of his local Caribbean island, it was revealed and accepted that he was not given a fair trial. His conviction was upheld, and his sentence was commuted to time served. After twenty-five years of wrongful imprisonment, Mr. Mawuli B. was "blessed to be free."

Keith Ernest Benjamin was raised on the beautiful St. Thomas, US Virgin Islands. Mr. Benjamin is a product of the public school system where he graduated from the Charlotte Amalie High School. He obtained his Bachelor of Arts Degree in Social Psychology from Champman University in Orange County, California. He currently holds the position of Assistant Director of Facilities Management at the Virgin Islands Legislature. In his spare time Mr. Benjamin enjoys carpentry, arts and craft and wood work. He also mentors at risk youths and participates in various public speaking engagements for the youths in his community. He believes that life is a journey and each individual has a story. Often times learning of other people's stories give us hope, faith, inspiration, fortitude and courage to never give up.

Xlibris